Momma, Where Are You From?

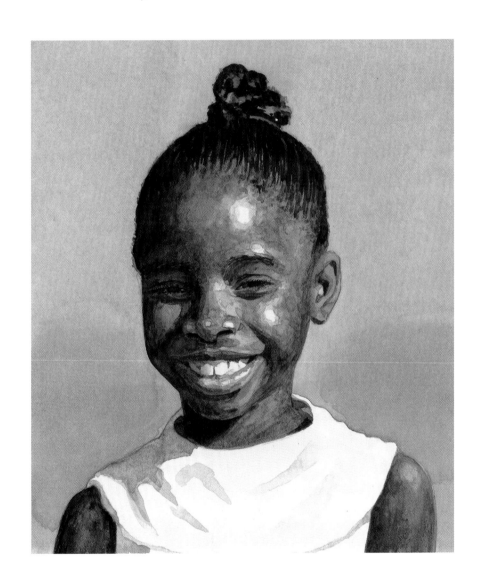

To Momma Joan (Stevenson).

For your support and dedication to children's literature and the arts. — C.K.S.

Text copyright © 2000 by Marie Bradby. Illustrations copyright © 2000 by Chris K. Soentpiet. All rights reserved. No part of this book may be reproduced or transmitted in any form or by any means, electronic or mechanical, including photocopying, recording, or by any information storage or retrieval system, without permission in writing from the Publisher. Orchard Books, A Grolier Company, 95 Madison Avenue, New York, NY 10016. Manufactured in the United States of America. Printed and bound by Phoenix Color Corp. Book design by Mina Greenstein.

The text of this book is set in 17 point Cochin Bold. The illustrations are watercolor. 10 9 8 7 6 5 4 3 2 1

Library of Congress Cataloging-in-Publication Data. Bradby, Marie. Momma, where are you from? / by Marie Bradby ; illustrated by Chris K. Soentpiet.   p.   cm.
Summary: Momma describes the special people and surroundings of her childhood, in a place where the edge of town met the countryside, in a time when all the children at school were brown. ISBN 0-531-30105-2 (trade : alk. paper).—ISBN 0-531-33105-9 (library : alk. paper)
[1. City and town life Fiction. 2. Afro-Americans Fiction. 3. Mother and child Fiction.] 1. Soentpiet, Chris K., ill. II. Title.
PZ7.B7175Mn 2000 [E]—dc21 99-23068

Momma, Where Are You From?

by MARIE BRADBY

illustrations by
CHRIS K. SOENTPIET

ORCHARD BOOKS   NEW YORK

Momma, where are you from?
Where are you from, Momma?

I'm from Monday mornings, washing loads of clothes in the wringer washer

**and peach baskets full of laundry to hang on the clothesline
strung from tree to tree—
the sun bleaching the sheets, the wind whipping them dry.**

I am from beans—green, lima, and pea—picked, strung, snapped, and shelled into pans,
then put on the stove to simmer for an hour.

I am from peddlers, driving a creaky old wagon with a big old horse and calling up and down the street:
"Fish-man! Fish-man! I've got fresh trout, spots, and croakers today! Fish-man! Fish-man!"

"When did you get them?" my mother would ask.
"They're real fresh. They came in the dock early this morning."
"All right," she'd say, "I'll take some croakers."

Calling: "Rag-man! Rag-man! Got any rags to sell?
Ten cents a pound!"
My mother would give him a bundle of worn-out
clothes and later stash the money in the cookie jar.

Calling: "Ice-man! Ice-man!"
If it was real hot, we would get two blocks of ice.
Momma would crack it with a pick and give me the
chips to suck on.

Momma, where is that place?
Where is that place, Momma?

It's where the edge of town met the countryside; where the city sidewalk ended and chickens ran through yards. Where families grew into a neighborhood as close as a knit sweater; where we threw up a hand to everyone we saw. Where I saw Miss Mary passing our house in the morning on her way to work and Mr. Thompson coming home from baking bread all night.

It's where the school bus took my older brothers and sister way across town past school . . . after school . . . after school . . . until it came to a school where all the children were brown— some light, some dark, some in-between.

Where days took their time and morning lay on the
rolling hills as long as she pleased.
Where I played under a gum ball tree that took up
the whole sky

and wondered why Miss Mary cleaned someone else's house, why the sidewalk ended at the edge of my neighborhood, and why my brothers and sister didn't go to the school right up the street.

Where afternoons, my brothers delivered newspapers, and I sprinkled and rolled up clothes, while my sister pressed with two flat irons—one to use, the other to heat up on the stove and be ready when the first went cold.

Where everything we wore and used was starched and ironed, even dish towels and underwear.

Where Friday evenings we fried fish outdoors,
and my cousins would come over with cherry pie and ice cream.
We would sit around tubs of iced sodas in the backyard, and
Daddy would say to Cousin Albert, "What'll you have?"

Where we children played "One-Two-Three Red Light,"
while the adults listened to ball games on the radio—
the Washington Senators and the Baltimore Orioles.
Where Daddy played his old Duke Ellington and Count
Basie records and we danced in the shadows, switching our
hips, popping our fingers, and pretending to be adults.

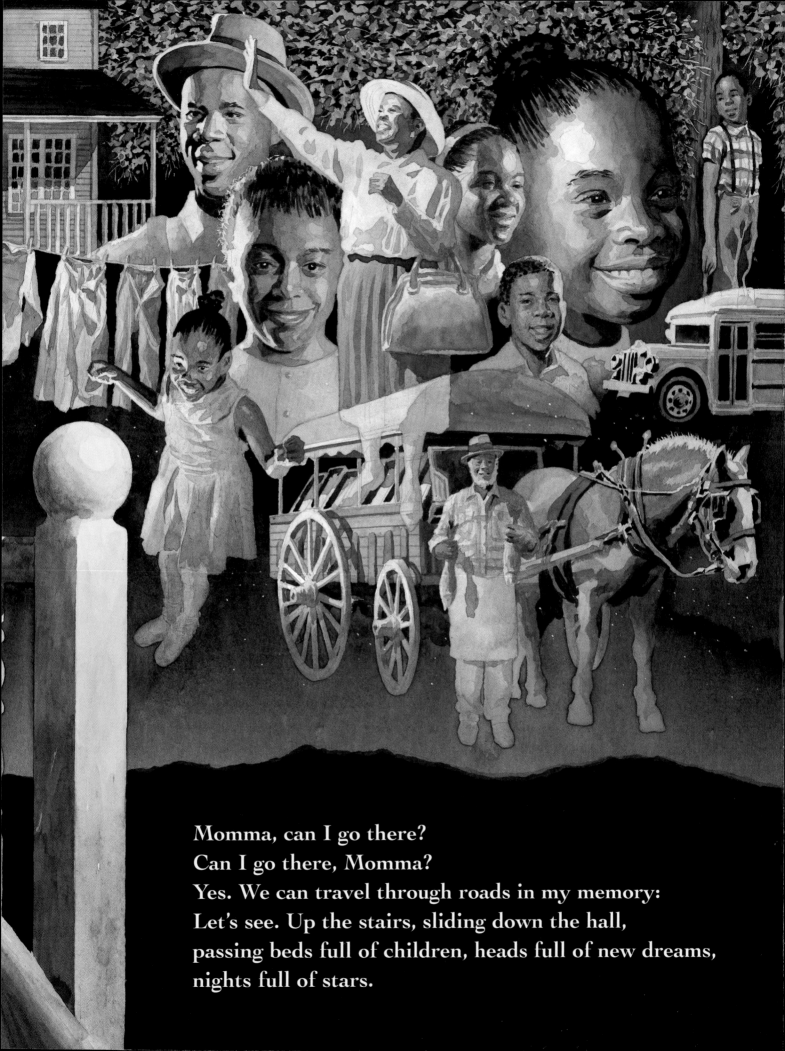

Momma, can I go there?
Can I go there, Momma?
Yes. We can travel through roads in my memory:
Let's see. Up the stairs, sliding down the hall,
passing beds full of children, heads full of new dreams,
nights full of stars.

Yes.
I am that morning-washing, bean-snapping, wagon-watching,
tree-swinging, Miss Mary–waving, brown bus–riding,
clothes-sprinkling, croaker-eating, Red Light–playing,
finger-popping, star-dreaming girl.
That's where I'm from.